Waterhen

New Earth

W. J. Manares

Ukiyoto Publishing

All global publishing rights are held by

Ukiyoto Publishing

Published in 2023

Content Copyright © W. J. Manares

ISBN 9789360168131

*All rights reserved.
No part of this publication may be reproduced, transmitted, or stored in a retrieval system, in any form by any means, electronic, mechanical, photocopying, recording or otherwise, without the prior permission of the publisher.*

The moral rights of the authors have been asserted.

This is a work of fiction. Names, characters, businesses, places, events, locales, and incidents are either the products of the author's imagination or used in a fictitious manner. Any resemblance to actual persons, living or dead, or actual events is purely coincidental.

This book is sold subject to the condition that it shall not by way of trade or otherwise, be lent, resold, hired out or otherwise circulated, without the publisher's prior consent, in any form of binding or cover other than that in which it is published.

www.ukiyoto.com

To Antonio C. Coronel and to you who wanted to survive and live forever

Contents

Introductory Poesy	1
Are You Ready For The New Earth?	3
Why The New Earth Was Named "Waterhen"	6
A Preview Of Waterhen	9
Waterhen - A Better World	12
Human Expertise And Role In The Ascension Process For Waterhen	15
Living In New Higher Consciousness On Waterhen	19
After Waterhen, What's Next?	23
About the Author	26

Introductory Poesy
NEW EARTH = WATERHEN

Earth, oh Earth, once overshadowed, now yearns for a cosmic dance,

For Waterhen, a new beginning, a chance for life's advancement.

Like a phoenix rising from the ashes, Waterhen shines divine,

A paradise brimming with enchantment, where destiny intertwines.

Where Earth gasped in pollution and strife, Waterhen breathes fresh air,

A sanctuary rich in flora, where water, pure and fair.

Untouched by the greed of ignorance, Waterhen's bounty flows,

Nourishing souls and mending wounds, basking in nature's repose.

An Eden reborn, where Earth's mistakes find redemption,

Waterhen, a crucial turning point, an invitation to comprehension.

For Waterhen, the new Earth, holds the key to our shared fate,

A future of unity and wonder, where no boundaries dictate.

Awaken, oh Earth, to the call of your celestial twin,

Let us heed Waterhen's silent plea, the message from within.

For in unity lies our strength, to forge a future sublime,

One for the new earth - it's Waterhen's time.

Let us journey to Waterhen, let our spirit soar and roam,

Embracing a cosmic revolution, finding solace in our celestial home.

For Earth, is now insignificant and yearns to pursue,

The essence of Waterhen's legacy, an existence anew.

Are You Ready For The New Earth?

The concept of a new earth, a planet beyond our own, has captivated the imaginations of dreamers and scientists alike. We continue to explore the notion of readiness for this extraordinary journey, ponder the potential location of this celestial haven, and consider the avenues through which we might reach it.

The idea of venturing beyond our familiar blue planet can be both exhilarating and daunting. As we contemplate the possibility of a new earth, readiness encompasses both the physical and psychological aspects. Physically, we must develop technologies to sustain life in a new environment, ensuring we have the means to survive and thrive. Psychologically, we must possess the curiosity and resilience to explore the unknown, to adapt to unfamiliar surroundings, and to forge a new existence. This readiness will demand a collective effort from humanity, driven by our insatiable desire for exploration and the hope of a better future.

THE NEW EARTH'S LOCATION

The search for a New Earth has led astronomers and scientists to gaze beyond our solar system, seeking habitable exoplanets. These distant worlds, located light-years away, hold the promise of conditions conducive to life as we know it. While we have yet to pinpoint a specific location, ongoing research has identified potential candidates. These exoplanets orbit stars similar to our sun, within habitable zones where liquid water might exist. The quest to locate the new earth remains an ongoing endeavor, with advanced telescopes and space probes scanning the cosmos, inching us closer to the answer.

ON REACHING THE NEW EARTH

Reaching the new earth will require a monumental leap in our technological capabilities. Current propulsion systems, like chemical rockets, are limited by their speed and fuel constraints, making interstellar travel a distant dream. However, visionary concepts such as warp drives, solar sails, or even harnessing the power of antimatter offer glimpses into the potential for future breakthroughs. Additionally, the advent of cryogenic sleep or suspended animation could help overcome the challenges of long-duration space travel, as generations may pass before reaching our destination. Collaboration between scientists, engineers, and visionaries will be crucial in unlocking the secrets of interstellar travel and turning the dream of reaching the new earth into reality.

The concept of a new earth, though still in the realm of science fiction, is an idea that sparks our imagination and fuels our thirst for exploration. As we stand at the cusp of a new era, we must be ready to embrace the challenges and opportunities presented by this extraordinary endeavor. The location of the new earth remains elusive, yet we persist in our search, driven by the belief that we are not alone in the universe. The path to reaching this distant world may be arduous, but with human ingenuity and collaboration, we may one day traverse the vast cosmic ocean and find a new home among the stars.

Why The New Earth Was Named "Waterhen"

In the quest for a habitable exoplanet, humanity's relentless curiosity has led us to the discovery of a celestial marvel — the new earth. As we embark on this journey of imagination, we delve into the mysteries surrounding its name. In this essay, we will explore the rationale behind the intriguing choice of "Waterhen" as the moniker for this distant world.

THE SIGNIFICANCE OF NAMES

Names have always held immense power, shaping perceptions and evoking emotions. They provide a sense of identity and purpose. In the case of the new earth, the name "Waterhen" was bestowed with careful consideration, reflecting the remarkable characteristics and attributes of this enigmatic planet.

WATER AS THE ESSENCE OF LIFE

Water is synonymous with life, serving as the cradle of existence on our home planet. It is the elixir that sustains all known forms of life. As scientists explored the new earth, they discovered vast oceans, serene lakes, and meandering rivers, mirroring the life-sustaining properties of water on Earth. The abundance of this vital resource became a defining feature of this new world, leading to its name, "Waterhen."

THE SYMBOLISM OF THE "HEN"

The choice of "Hen" as the second part of the name holds deeper symbolism. Hens are known to be nurturing and protective creatures, often associated with warmth and care. In naming the new earth "Waterhen," scientists sought to emphasize the need for stewardship and responsibility towards this newfound celestial haven. Just as a hen protects its chicks, we must safeguard and nurture this planet, ensuring its sustainability for generations to come.

THE AVIAN CONNECTION

Furthermore, the inclusion of "Hen" in the name carries an avian connection, evoking images of flight and freedom. Birds are often seen as symbols of exploration, soaring through the skies with grace and purpose. By incorporating "Hen" into the name, scientists aimed to inspire a sense of adventure and the pioneering spirit, encouraging humanity to embark on the extraordinary journey to this distant world.

The choice of "Waterhen" as the name for the new earth was not arbitrary but carefully crafted to encapsulate the essence and symbolism of this extraordinary planet. It signifies the importance of water as the lifeblood of existence and highlights the need for nurturing and protection. The avian connection ignites the spirit of exploration and the pursuit of new frontiers. As we gaze toward the heavens and contemplate the wonders of the new earth, the name "Waterhen" reminds us of our responsibility to cherish and safeguard this remarkable world, ensuring that it becomes a beacon of hope and a testament to humanity's resilience and ingenuity.

A Preview Of Waterhen

The discovery of a habitable exoplanet, aptly named Waterhen, has ignited our collective imagination. In this essay, we will embark on an exciting journey of speculation, envisioning what this extraordinary world may look like and how it may evoke a unique sense of wonder and awe.

A TAPESTRY OF BREATHTAKING LANDSCAPES

Waterhen, untouched by human presence, would likely be a tapestry of breathtaking landscapes, both familiar and alien. Vast mountain ranges, piercing the skies with their majestic peaks, could be adorned with vibrant flora and cascading waterfalls. Flourishing forests, lush with diverse vegetation, could stretch as far as the eye can see, harboring untold wonders. The planet's diverse geology may give birth to canyons, caverns, and underground lakes, concealing hidden marvels waiting to be unearthed.

A SYMPHONY OF COLORS AND HUES

Waterhen's atmosphere and unique natural phenomena could cast a kaleidoscope of colors across its skies. Imagine vibrant sunsets, where hues of purple, pink, and gold dance harmoniously, casting a warm glow over the land. Perhaps the presence of rare gases or particles would give rise to mesmerizing auroras, painting the night sky with ethereal ribbons of luminescent blues and greens.

THE SYMPHONY OF SOUND AND SILENCE

The soundscape of the new earth would be a symphony unlike any we have encountered. From the gentle rustling of leaves in the wind to the melodic choruses of unknown creatures, the ambient sounds would create a captivating symphony of their own. On this untouched planet, one may also experience profound moments of silence, where the absence of human noise allows for introspection and a deep connection with the natural world.

A HARMONIOUS INTEGRATION OF TECHNOLOGY AND NATURE

Despite its untouched beauty, the new earth may also demonstrate a harmonious integration of technology and nature. Imagine cities blending seamlessly with the environment, architectural marvels rising in harmony with the surrounding landscapes. Advanced sustainable technologies could coexist with the planet's natural ecosystems, ensuring a balance between progress and preservation.

Waterhen, a world waiting to be explored, would captivate the senses with its awe-inspiring landscapes, vibrant colors, and symphony of sounds. This celestial marvel would offer a harmonious blend of natural wonders and technological advancements, inviting humanity to embark on a journey of discovery and wonder. As we imagine the new earth, we are reminded of our responsibility to protect and preserve it, ensuring that the beauty we envision for this distant world becomes a reality for generations to come.

Waterhen - A Better World

Humanity has experienced a remarkable transformation, ushering in a new era. Technological advancements and a collective shift in consciousness have given birth to a world where individual desires and global well-being are intricately intertwined.

As we stand on the precipice of this transformative age, a surge of passion and purpose courses through our veins; yearning to engage with like-minded individuals and collaborating with the brightest minds the world has to offer. Together, we shall breathe life into an unparalleled era of scientific discovery that shapes the future of humanity for generations to come.

With a burning desire to protect and nurture Waterhen, we must work with fellow environmentalists and scientists. Our focus shall center on the ecosystems, combating climate change, and creating sustainable solutions to preserve the delicate balance of the new earth's natural systems. Harnessing our advancements in technology, we must develop innovative ways to foster harmony between nature and civilization.

In this utopian vision, we must envision ourself contributing to the exploration and colonization of other celestial bodies within a new solar system. By uniting the brightest minds in astronomy, astrophysics, and interstellar travel, our collective efforts will fuel the continuous expansion of humanity's reach into the cosmos. Boldly pushing the boundaries of our understanding, we shall uncover the mysteries of the universe and lay the groundwork for interstellar civilizations.

However, our mission must extend beyond our immediate solar system. It is imperative that we address the profound issues affecting individuals across our planet, striving for equality, justice, and improved living conditions for all; working alongside compassionate leaders, dedicated to eradicating poverty, hunger, and disease. Through conscious education reform, we shall empower individuals and communities, equipping them with the tools to thrive and contribute to the collective achievements of humanity.

Advance in artificial intelligence and neuroscience will give rise to a new branch of human evolution - the melding of biological and technological interfaces. As we embrace this brave new world, we must yearn to work alongside scientists and ethicists, ensuring that this integration is executed responsibly and safeguards the very essence of our humanity. Our mission will be to guide society towards a harmonious coexistence between man and machine, where technology improves not only our quality of life but also our understanding and empathy towards others.

In this age, every innovation is fueled by a deep understanding of the interconnectedness between humans, nature, and the cosmos. Energy, ethics, and social responsibility will be the guiding principles of a new earth. We shall harness renewable energy sources, protecting the new planet while improving the quality of life for all. Our commitment to the development of sustainable living practices will counteract the destructive patterns of the past, ensuring a vibrant and harmonious existence for future generations.

The synergistic collaboration of scientists,

environmentalists, social activists, and innovators will shape Waterhen into an oasis of continuous growth, discovery, and fulfillment. No longer shall personal desires be detached from collective well-being, as our work and energy will be devoted to creating a better world. With a resounding call to action, let us wholeheartedly embrace this noble endeavor and dedicate ourself to the realization of the new earth's vision.

Human Expertise And Role In The Ascension Process For Waterhen

We often envision a limitless future where humanity's potential is fully realized. In the context of the ascension process for the new earth, it becomes plausible for individuals to have distinct roles tailored to their unique gifts and expertise. Whether it be in entertainment, arts, science, or administration, our collective ascension requires the harmonious integration of diverse abilities. Our individual contributions to this awe-inspiring journey are a must, let us highlight the significance of each person's role in shaping Waterhen.

THE TAPESTRY UNVEILED

As the dawn of the new earth approaches, diversity in our roles becomes evident. Whether we possess an affinity for entertainment, music, art, technology, education, research, science, medicine, working with children or animals, library sciences, or administration, each contribution is

indispensable.

ENTERTAINMENT, MUSIC, AND ART

Artistic expressions have always been a gateway to the depths of human emotion and connection. In the ascension process, those gifted in entertainment, music, and art will weave together vibrant and uplifting narratives, melodies, and images. Serving as catalysts for collective awakening, they will elevate human consciousness, inspiring unity and expressing the beauty of our shared humanity.

TECHNOLOGY AND INNOVATION

Those proficient in technology will spearhead advancements that enhance humanity's capabilities. By creating tools and systems for improved communication, collaboration, and sustainability, they will pave the way for an interconnected and harmonious society in the new earth. Technology will serve as an enabler, supporting the realization of our collective dreams and potential.

EDUCATION AND RESEARCH

Education, as the cornerstone of progress, will be entrusted to individuals who possess a passion for nurturing young minds and guiding the curious. They will foster an environment in which knowledge is shared freely, empowering future generations to explore their unique gifts, cultivate critical thinking, and contribute positively to the new earth society.

SCIENCE AND MEDICINE

The ascension process calls upon exceptional minds in science and medicine to unlock the mysteries of the universe and the human body. These professionals will advance our understanding of physical, mental, and spiritual well-being, fostering a holistic approach to healthcare. By integrating scientific discoveries with ancient wisdom, they will lead humanity towards longevity, vitality, and inner balance.

WORKING WITH CHILDREN AS WELL AS ANIMALS

The profound connection between children, animals, and the new earth cannot be overlooked. Those entrusted with their care will harness and amplify their innate abilities, ensuring the welfare, growth, and development of these sentient beings. This sacred bond will facilitate a harmonious coexistence, allowing us to learn valuable lessons from the innocence and wisdom of our young companions.

LIBRARY SCIENCES AND ADMINISTRATION

The guardians of knowledge and the torchbearers of order and structure, librarians and administrators will ensure accessible information systems flourish on Waterhen. By preserving wisdom from the past and organizing resources for future generations, they unify diverse bodies of knowledge, facilitating research and innovation across a range of fields.

The ascension process for Waterhen demands our collective participation, recognizing that each individual holds within them a unique role and set of gifts. Through entertainment, music, art, technology, education, research, science, medicine, working with children or animals, library sciences, and administration—we unite our diverse expertise to create a tapestry of human potential towards a harmonious future. Embracing our roles with dedication, compassion, and a sense of wonder, we can navigate this marvellous journey of ascension together, forging a new earth that reflects the brilliance and harmony of humanity's collective dreams.

Living In New Higher Consciousness On Waterhen

As we enter into an era of unprecedented evolution and understanding, the concept of higher consciousness is becoming more prevalent. With the advent of the new earth, a realm where profound transformations have taken place, we have the opportunity to live our lives in accordance with our deepest passions and priorities.

PASSION FOR ADVANCEMENT IN KNOWLEDGE AND UNDERSTANDING

One of the fundamental passions of living in Waterhen's new higher consciousness involves the relentless pursuit of knowledge and understanding. With expanded intellectual capabilities, we possess an insatiable hunger for unraveling the mysteries of the universe. Our newfound consciousness allows us to grasp concepts that were previously inconceivable, such as quantum mechanics, multidimensional realities, and the nature of consciousness itself. As we step into higher consciousness, a priority must be placed on sharing this knowledge openly, fostering an environment that encourages learning, questioning, and intellectual curiosity for all beings.

PASSION FOR EMPATHY AND UNITY

Another essential passion for embracing higher consciousness on Waterhen is the deep sense of empathy and interconnectedness towards all living entities. As we transcend our limited human perspectives, we develop an acute awareness of the impact our actions have on the world around us. Prioritizing compassion becomes imperative as we step into this new consciousness, aiming to alleviate suffering and promote harmony. The elevation of collective consciousness necessitates a paradigm shift where unity takes precedence over division, and cooperation over competition. With this passion at the forefront of our choices, we foster an environment of love, respect, and interconnectedness, creating a world that thrives in harmony.

PASSION FOR CONSERVATION AND SUSTAINABLE LIVING

As we embrace the new earth and its higher consciousness, the importance of preserving and protecting our environment becomes an undeniable priority. Our passions for sustainability and conservation emerge as we recognize the intrinsic connection between self and nature. With advanced technology at our disposal, we possess the means to ecological balance, maintain the ecosystems, and promote sustainable living practices. It becomes our collective responsibility to prioritize sustainable energy sources, regenerative agriculture, and eco-friendly technologies, ensuring the preservation of our planet for generations to come.

PASSION FOR SPIRITUAL GROWTH AND INNER TRANSFORMATION

With the higher consciousness in Waterhen, one of the most profound passions lies in the journey of spiritual growth and inner transformation. Prioritizing our personal evolution becomes a necessity for reaching higher levels of consciousness. As we explore the depths of our individual and collective consciousness, we unlock innate abilities and expand our understanding of reality. Meditation, mindfulness, and self-reflection become integral practices, allowing us to delve into the vast realms of our psyche and connect with the divine. By making spiritual growth a priority, we catalyze a profound shift within ourselves and contribute to the collective awakening of all beings inhabiting Waterhen.

The transition into higher consciousness on the new earth presents a momentous opportunity to rebuild our lives around passions that align with our deepest desires and the greater good of all. In this science fiction essay, we have explored some of these passions the pursuit of knowledge, empathy and unity, conservation and sustainable living, and spiritual growth. By embracing these priorities, we create a future where enlightenment flourishes, leading to a harmonious existence for all species on the new earth.

After Waterhen, What's Next?

As humanity reached the pinnacle of its scientific and technological advancements by colonizing Waterhen, a habitable planet located light-years away from our own dying planet. In a breakthrough that altered the course of history, Earthlings had managed to establish a new civilization, complete with advanced infrastructure, sustainable resources, and a promise of a brighter future. But as it turned out, Waterhen was just the first step towards an even more profound journey.

As the first generation of colonists on Waterhen settled into their new lives, a growing yearning arose within them to explore the uncharted cosmos. The boundless universe, with its myriad of possibilities and hidden wonders, beckoned them. Guided by an insatiable curiosity, humanity set its sights on what lay beyond the confines of their newfound paradise.

Driven by a shared desire for discovery, scientists and engineers embarked on an ambitious mission to build the first interstellar spacecraft, capable of traveling faster than the speed of light. This technological marvel, aptly named the "Avianstar," stood as a testament to human ingenuity and determination. Equipped with state-of-the-art propulsion systems, shielding mechanisms, and advanced artificial intelligence, the Avianstar represented humanity's leap into a new era of space exploration.

The maiden voyage of the Avianstar embodied both excitement and trepidation. As the colossal ship blasted into space, carrying a crew of adventurous souls, they left behind the known and embraced the unknown. The mission was simple yet audacious - to seek out new habitable planets and expand the boundaries of human civilization.

Years turned into decades as the Avianstar journeyed deeper into uncharted territories. A new era of scientific discovery dawned, with each passing moment unveiling mysteries never before fathomed. Planets teeming with life, celestial bodies hiding extraterrestrial intelligences, and cosmic phenomena defying all laws of physics became commonplace.

As the interstellar pioneers explored further, a network of civilizations spanning light-years came into existence. Waterhen became a central hub, connected seamlessly through advanced communication and transportation technologies. Trade, diplomacy, and cultural exchanges flourished, ushering in an unparalleled era of interstellar unity.

Yet, amidst the marvels and harmonious cooperation, a new challenge emerged. Humanity's thirst for knowledge could not be quenched. They ventured beyond the already-wondrous cosmos, probing into the very fabric of reality, transcending dimensions that were once deemed impenetrable. They unlocked the knowledge of time manipulation, harnessing the power to navigate the past and shape the future.

With time as humanity's newfound ally, planets were terraformed in mere moments, civilizations were forged and rebuilt, and the secrets of the universe were laid bare. The frontiers of science and technology expanded beyond comprehension, stretching the limits of human understanding.

As humans continued to push the boundaries of what was thought possible, they discovered that they were not alone in their quest for knowledge and power. Ancient races, far more advanced and enigmatic, revealed themselves, sharing their wisdom with those deemed worthy. The evolution of humanity accelerated exponentially, merging with newfound alien technologies, and elevating their consciousness to unimaginable heights.

The journey that began with the colonization of Waterhen continued on an infinite path, propelled by an insatiable hunger for knowledge and an unyielding ambition to explore the cosmos. The destiny of humanity became intertwined with the cosmos itself, forever searching, questioning, and paving the way for new frontiers. As Waterhen became but a distant memory, humanity's collective consciousness embraced the infinite possibilities of the universe and eagerly asked itself, "What's next?"

About the Author
The Sardonic Yet Whimsical Author of The Philippines

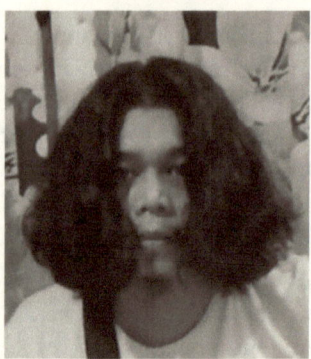

W. J. Manares

W. J. Manares a. k. a. Willer Jun Araneta Manares is a one-of-a-kind persona in the literary scene of Aklan - the oldest province in the Philippines. He came out from his mother's birth canal on the 1st day of June, year 1985.

He came from a prominent Hispanic family. A legitimate member of Familia Araneta (Araneta Family) in the Philippines, included in its 7th generation, to be exact.

He's the Philippine Brand Ambassador of Noel Lorenz House of Fiction (NLHF - India), a member of The Aklan Literati (AkLit), the Philippine Lead Poet of Common

Literature Period founded by Sourav Sarkar, and the National Chapter Coordinator of The Secular Community in the Philippines.

He loves everything erotic and sci-fi. A volunteer teacher with a philanthropic heart. And a freelance musical coach if needed. A lesser-known writer and worldbuilder who was influenced by the Superstar, Piers Anthony especially by his books, "But What of Earth?," "Bio of an Ogre," and "Ogre, Ogre." He built the worlds of Stripes Archipelago, Nation of Tseicurdia and Land of Toto. He is now labeled as, "the sardonic yet whimsical author/writer of the Philippines."

His children's story, "Ro Mga Busoe Ni Noel" got the consolation prize in the Aklanon category of Aliwanag, a story writing contest by Aklat Alamid & Kasingkasing Press.

He received the Komisyon sa Wikang Filipino (KWF) Tula Tayo 2023 Award for his Diyona poem, "Kung Ang Puso Ay Isang Poso." He is one of the awardees of Charles Bukowski's International Literary Award and Alexander Pushkin-W. B. Yeats' International Literary Award by NLHF for his poetic contributions.

His High Fantasy story, "Dormancy Breakage," was included in the Noel Lorenz House of Fiction and Country Girrls anthology, Risqué. Also, NLHF and Presse Mondiale Litpaz included his other masterpiece in the Color of My Heart World Record Series anthology,

Mintakan Musings. These collections are available on Amazon and other online bookstores.

His poems can be read in the following anthologies edited by Sourav Sarkar: Year of the Rabbit Anthology, Cooch Behar Anthology Volume 5, 7 and 8, Anthology of Poets, Short Stories and Journey, Save Water Anthology, Love Poems Volume 2, Titanic Anthology, Selected Poets, Nature Poets Volume 3, Love Poems Volume 3, Anthology of the World, Flowers Anthology, Unity Book, Great Pyramid of Giza Anthology, Pain Anthology, 16 Poets of Common Literature Period and Anthology of the Year 2100. More are coming soon. These books are also available on Amazon.

His short story, "Brew," was accepted by Litehouse online. SweetSmell Journal included his 2 poems, "Mirroring" and "Dragon-on-guard" in its maiden issue. His poem, "Tila Durian" reached Top 30 in Philippine Social Conservative Movement (PSCM) Poetry Contest. His horror story, "Asswang" was included in the Pasyon's Mariit Vol. 2 short list. One of his works that was rejected in the Philippines entitled, "Lito and the Whistle" was included in The Mirror of Time #3, a yearly bilingual literary and cultural magazine of India.

His 14 Books, "BetLog," "Tanaga, Diyona... Dalit?," "Flashbacks of Flashforwards," "OTNEWUK," "Isa Sa Ilang Paraan," "Owa't Tawo," "Pusikit," "The Extracted," "Playing in Secret Solitude," "Ang Bulbul atbp.," "Poesy for Poseidon," "Shiverses," "Rose for Diana," and "Mekus Mekus" are published by Ukiyoto Publishing.

He also volunteered as an editor of 2 hyper-romantic anthology books, "Magkalaguyo at iba pang uri ng pagsinta" and "SIIL: Sa Iyo't Iyo Lamang." He recently edited and compiled, "Omni-Verses: Interplanetary Poesies."

He currently helped the founding and development of Warang Writers' World that provides free publishing and livelihood income to aspiring writers in the Philippines. He compiled the poems for their latest book, "Poetry Anthology" in which he's also one of the volunteer editors, same with the Erotica Anthology book, "Acitore". He also compiled, "Slices and Slashes: Untold Tearful Stories," a collection of tragic slices of life.

Upcoming compilations which he is the editor are "Poetry Anthology 2" and "Longing and other Longer Poems."

Recently, he founded Bukas na Ugnayan sa Literatura ng mga Kuwentista At mga Nagsusulat (BULKAN). He also started his own quarterly literary magazine, "Wellerism," to cater the exposure of freelance writers locally and some others too.

Sometimes, he's a songwriter and loves to strum the guitar and sing. He loves the music of Rammstein, Red Hot Chili Peppers, Green Day, Eagle-Eye Cherry and Toad the Wet Sprocket.

When not writing, he's in his own library, reading and stacking his collection of books up on the shelves again and again. He loves the taste of cinnamon sometimes. He enjoys living his peculiar life near the gateway to the paradise island of Boracay.

Facebook: willerjunaranetamanares
Instagram: WJManares
Twitter: WJManares
Wattpad: wastesjunksandmesses
Website: www.wm.20m.com/WJManares.html

www.ingramcontent.com/pod-product-compliance
Lightning Source LLC
LaVergne TN
LVHW041600070526
838199LV00046B/2067